UP DOWN

ऊपर नीचे

Vinayak Varma विनायक वर्मा

Translated by Deeya Nayar अनुवाद दीया नायर

Tulika

Appu wanted to play on the seesaw.
He asked a grasshopper,
"Will you play with me?"

अप्पू सीसॉ पर खेलना चाहता था।
उसने एक टिड्डे से पूछा,
"तुम मेरे साथ खेलोगे?"

The grasshopper sat on one side.
Appu sat on the other side.
Down came the seesaw. Up went the grasshopper.

टिड्डा एक तरफ़ बैठा।
अप्पू दूसरी तरफ़ बैठा।
नीचे आया सीसॉ। ऊपर गया टिड्डा।

"You're too heavy!" said the grasshopper.

"तुम बहुत भारी हो!" टिड्डा बोला।

Appu asked a mouse, "Will you play with me?"

अप्पू ने एक चूहे से पूछा, "तुम मेरे साथ खेलोगे?"

The mouse sat on one side.
Appu sat on the other side.
Down came the seesaw. Up went the mouse.

चूहा एक तरफ़ बैठा।
अप्पू दूसरी तरफ़ बैठा।
नीचे आया सीसॉ। ऊपर गया चूहा।

"You're too heavy!" said the mouse.

"तुम बहुत भारी हो!" चूहा बोला।

Appu asked a dog, "Will you play with me?"

अप्पू ने एक कुत्ते से पूछा, "तुम मेरे साथ खेलोगे?"

The dog sat on one side. Appu sat on the other side.
Down came the seesaw. Up went the dog.

कुत्ता एक तरफ़ बैठा। अप्पू दूसरी तरफ़ बैठा।
नीचे आया सीसॉ। ऊपर गया कुत्ता।

"You're too heavy!" said the dog.

"तुम बहुत भारी हो!" कुत्ता बोला।

Appu asked a cow, "Will you play with me?"

अप्पू ने एक गाय से पूछा, "तुम मेरे साथ खेलोगी?"

Appu sat on one side.
The cow sat on the other side.
Down came the seesaw. Up went Appu.

अप्पू एक तरफ़ बैठा।
गाय दूसरी तरफ़ बैठी।
नीचे आया सीसॉ। ऊपर गया अप्पू।

"You're too light!" said the cow.

"तुम बहुत हल्के हो!" गाय बोली।

Appu lay on the grass. A little girl came running to him. "Will you play with me?" she asked.

अप्पू घास पर लेट गया। एक छोटी लड़की उसके पास दौड़कर आई। "तुम मेरे साथ खेलोगे?" उसने पूछा।

She sat on one side.
Appu sat on the other side.
Up down. Up down. Up down.
They both played for a long time.

वह एक तरफ़ बैठी।
अप्पू दूसरी तरफ़ बैठा।
ऊपर नीचे। ऊपर नीचे। ऊपर नीचे।
दोनों बहुत देर तक खेलते रहे।